The author is a 35-year-old mum to Scarlett. Married and living in Stoke-on-Trent. Has two golden retrievers and enjoys reading and going on adventures with my little family.

CARLY DUTTON

SCARLETT
SHABBEE

THE ADVENTURE BEGINS

AUSTIN MACAULEY PUBLISHERS™

LONDON * CAMBRIDGE * NEW YORK * SHARJAH

Copyright © Carly Dutton (2020)

A CIP catalogue record for this title is available from the British Library.

ISBN 9781528988063 (Paperback)
ISBN 9781528990158 (ePub e-book)

www.austinmacauley.com

First Published (2020)
Austin Macauley Publishers Ltd
25 Canada Square
Canary Wharf
London
E14 5LQ

Dedicated to my husband, my parents and my little inspiration, Scarlett.

This is a story about a little girl called Scarlett and a new magical friend.

Scarlett was an only child; this could often get boring and a bit lonely. One day Scarlett went on holiday to Cornwall with her mummy and daddy.

They went to a place called St Ives; it was absolutely stunning. Every day, they walked into the town for cornish pasties, cream teas and ice cream. They went to the beach most days and enjoyed the sunshine and making sand castles.

One day however, it started to rain while they were on the beach—big heavy rain drops that seemed to appear from nowhere! They decided to take shelter in the arcade just off the beach. The arcade was busy and noisy and there were games everywhere.

Scarlett and her parents played on a few of the games whilst waiting for the rain to pass. Scarlett spotted a machine filled with toys. Amongst the toys there was a beautiful unicorn; it was purple with big brown eyes, and pink patches either side of its body and a golden horn on top of its head. It looked so magical.

Scarlett couldn't take her eyes off the unicorn, and did she just see the unicorn smile at her?

Pulling her parents to the machine, she pointed at the toy and looked hopefully up at her daddy.

After a few tries, the machine picked the unicorn up! Scarlett couldn't believe her luck. The unicorn's horn shone (only for a few seconds) but long enough for Scarlett to see.

The unicorn dropped into the tray and Scarlett's daddy handed it to her.

"What will you call her Scarlett?"

"Shabbee" – (pronounced like Shabby) was Scarlett's reply.

Suddenly, it had stopped raining, so they decided to walk back to their cottage with Scarlett hugging Shabbee all the way.

Scarlett spent a happy afternoon playing with her new unicorn Shabbee, she was so fluffy and magical looking.

Scarlett chatted away to her new toy and the unicorn smiled at her again.

"Can you hear me?" Scarlett asked.

The unicorns horn shone again and a bright golden flash of colour filled the room.

Scarlett knew there was something very special about this unicorn and she didn't feel quite so lonely talking to her new toy.

Scarlett was right, this was a magical unicorn, little did Scarlett know quite how magical Shabbee was and all the adventures they would have together.

Scarlett had heard that there were sea lions down by the harbour, but by the time Scarlett, her mummy and daddy had got there, they had gone.

Scarlett was so upset; she had never seen a sea lion before.

"Scarlett"… Who said that?

"Scarlett"… There it was again! Scarlett looked around but couldn't see anyone but her unicorn Shabbee.

"Was that you" Scarlett asked.

"Yes, I can speak to you" replied the unicorn.

"I heard you were upset because you didn't get to see the sea lions"

"I am, I've never seen one before" Scarlett said sadly.

"That's okay; I can take you to where they live, just press your nose and say bop"

Scarlett laughed and pressed her nose "BOP" she shouted.

They were suddenly transported to lots of rocks where big brown creatures lay about.

"They don't look anything like I thought they would" giggled Scarlett.

Scarlett wanted to get closer but Shabbee stopped her.

"Remember Scarlett, they are wild animals and we're in their home, so we don't know how they'll react."

Suddenly, Scarlett saw a baby seal thrashing about in the water, something was caught on him, and it looked like a large piece of plastic.

Scarlett was worried and felt helpless but she needn't have worried for long because out of nowhere a life boat appeared. The crew on the lifeboat carefully managed to get the bit of plastic off the baby sea lion and he returned to his mother happy once again.

"It's lucky, the life boat came along when it did, but they may not always be around to help, that's why we must always throw away our rubbish especially when we visit the beach" Shabbee said to Scarlett.

It was time Scarlett and Shabbee went home; it was starting to get dark.

"Remember what we do Scarlett, press your nose and say BOP." "BOP" they both shouted.

Scarlett was back in her room with Shabbee. Shabbee went very still again but still smiled a small knowing smile.

Scarlett's mummy came up to see her.

"I'm sorry we didn't get to see the Sea Lions today Scarlett, maybe another day"

Scarlett just smiled, if only mummy knew!

Scarlett knew this wasn't the first adventure she would have with Shabbee, the magical unicorn. She had a feeling there was going to be many more...